GAME OF THRONES
HOUSE OF THE DRAGON

THE OFFICIAL COLOURING BOOK

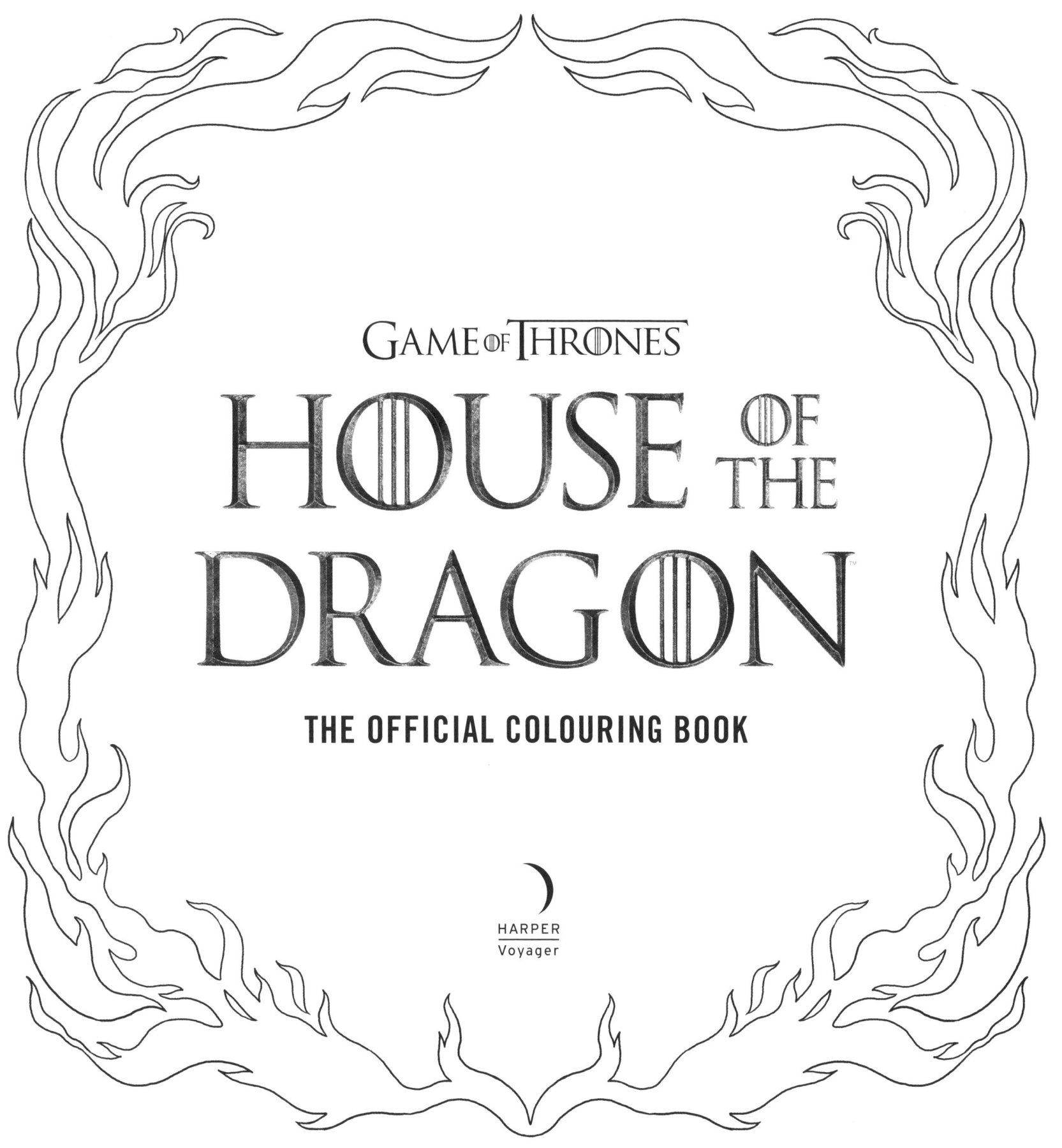

A Random House Worlds Trade Paperback Original

 Copyright © 2024 Home Box Office, Inc. GAME OF THRONES and all related characters and elements © & ™ Home Box Office, Inc. WB SHIELD: ™ & © WBEI (s24)

All rights reserved.

Harper*Voyager*
An imprint of HarperCollins*Publishers* Ltd,
1 London Bridge Street, London SE1 9GF

www.harpercollins.co.uk

HarperCollins*Publishers*
Macken House, 39/40 Mayor Street Upper,
Dublin 1, D01 C9W8, Ireland

First published by HarperCollins*Publishers* Ltd 2024
1

This edition published by arrangement with Random House Worlds,
an imprint of Random House, a division of Penguin Random House LLC.

Random House is a registered trademark, and Random House Worlds and colophon are trademarks of Penguin Random House LLC.

A catalogue record for this book is available from the British Library.

ISBN 978-0-00-871970-8

Printed and bound in Italy by ROTOLITO S.p.A.

Illustrations: Tomislav Tomić

Editor: Matt Belford
Editorial assistant: Lydia Estrada
Production editor: Serena Wang
Art director and designer: Debbie Berne
Production manager: Dustin Amick

All rights reserved. No part of this publication may be reproduced, stored in a retrieval system, or transmitted, in any form or by any means, electronic, mechanical, photocopying, recording or otherwise, without the prior permission of the publishers.

This book contains FSC™ certified paper and other controlled sources
to ensure responsible forest management.

For more information visit: www.harpercollins.co.uk/green